EMERY
THE EXPLORER
A Jungle Adventure
By Louise John

FICTION
EXPRESS

Contents

Chapter 1

A Mysterious Map

For as long as he could remember, Emery had liked finding lost things. He was actually very good at it. When Mum lost her keys, Emery found them in the garden. When Dad lost his sock, Emery found it under the bed.

Soon, Emery wanted to find more interesting things. He wanted to solve mysteries and discover secret places. He dreamed of hidden treasures. Now Emery was the best explorer in the country. If there was treasure to be found, Emery would find it.

One frosty winter morning, Emery sat munching his toast. He was reading *Explorer Weekly* magazine and dreaming of exciting places. His pet monkey, Spider, suddenly let out a screech. It was the postman arriving.

"Hey, Spider, fetch the post for me!" cried Emery.

Spider sighed grumpily. He ran to the door and picked up the letters. *Why did humans always expect animals to fetch things?* he thought to himself.

"It's a package from the professor!" said Emery. He ripped the big brown envelope open.

A torn piece of paper fell to the floor. Spider picked it up. He looked at it and scratched his head. He turned it the other way up. Then he leapt onto Emery's shoulder.

Emery took the piece of paper. "It's a map, Spider!" he said, excitedly. "Well, half a map. It's torn down the middle. I wonder where the other half is?"

Spider hopped up and down and chattered in excitement. A map would mean only one thing – another adventure!

"There's a note, too," said Emery. He read it quickly. "It has some good news and some bad news...."

Chapter 2

A Race Against Time

Spider tilted his head to one side to listen as Emery read out the note.

"The good news is that we're going on a jungle expedition to find some treasure – the missing yellow diamond of the Amazon, to be precise. The bad news is that Dex has the other half of our map…."

"Ooh, ooh, ah!" gibbered Spider, doing a somersault onto the table. He was thinking about Dex. Dex had a mean mouth and angry eyebrows. Spider had nipped him once. He didn't taste nice at all.

Dex D Saster was Emery's biggest rival. He was trouble with a capital T. He always did his best to ruin Emery's adventures. Why did *he* have the other half of the map? One thing was for sure – he'd be looking for the treasure as soon as he could. It was going to be a race against time.

"Come on, Spider!" yelled Emery. "We're off to the jungle. We need to find the other half of that map.…"

* * *

Emery put on his explorer's clothes. He filled his rucksack. "Toothbrush…camping stove… tent…that should do it."

I hope there are some bananas in there, Spider grunted to himself.

Emery left a note on the kitchen table for his parents:

Gone exploring. Back soon.
Love E xxx

The very next afternoon, Emery and Spider were on a small plane, swooping over the Amazon jungle. Lush green trees stretched as far as their eyes could see. The weather was hot and steamy.

"Are we nearly there yet?" Emery asked the pilot, as the plane turned sharply to the left. It began heading downwards. Then something awful happened....

Chapter 3

A Close Shave

The pilot turned around in his seat. He gave Emery and Spider a cheery wave. "Just heading in to land, now," he winked at Emery.

"D…D…D…Dex?" gasped Emery, confused. "You! Wha… what are you doing flying our plane?"

Spider gibbered angrily. He let out a furious howl. Before Dex could answer, Spider jumped up onto the villain's shoulders and nipped his ear. He covered Dex's eyes with his paws.

"Yee-ouch! Get off me, you silly monkey, I can't see!" Dex stood up with a yelp. He flapped his arms around, trying to get Spider off his neck.

Without a pilot at the controls, the nose of the plane dipped. It started to dive towards the ground at full speed.

"We're going to crash!" yelled Emery. He ran to the cockpit and took hold of the control stick. He pulled it back towards him with all his strength. "Come on, come on," he muttered. "Up you come."

Slowly the nose of the plane rose. Then Emery brought it to a smooth landing in a gap in the trees. He let out his breath. "Phew, that was a close shave!"

Behind him, Dex was still struggling with Spider. "Emery, call your stupid pet off me!" shouted Dex.

"Ooh, ah!" shrieked Spider. *How dare he call me stupid?*

Dex flung himself backwards, trying to push Spider off. He cracked his head on the side of the cockpit door and slumped to the floor in a daze.

Chapter 4

The Wobbly Bridge

Emery looked down at his arch-enemy.

"Good work, Spider!" he grinned. "Looks as if Dex is having a little snooze. Quick, we need to find his half of the map before he wakes up!"

Emery and Spider stepped out of the plane into the steamy jungle. They emptied Dex's rucksack onto the ground. The sun beat down on their heads.

"Hmm… compass, penknife, mosquito net, water bottle, banana…" muttered Emery.

Spider smiled. Quick as a flash, he grabbed the banana and scampered up the nearest tree. Hiding behind a big leaf, he peeled back the skin and quickly gobbled up the fruit.

"Here's the map!" exclaimed Emery. He held the two halves together. They fitted perfectly. "Come on, Spider, let's get a head start before he wakes up! Looks as if we need to head south to find the swinging bridge over the Inca Waterfall...."

Emery and Spider set off. They made their way through the thick undergrowth of the jungle. There were noises of different insects and animals all around them. Spider howled excitedly to answer the calls of other monkeys on the way.

Before long, they arrived at the swinging bridge. It stretched out over the dazzling water of the magnificent waterfall. The bridge was old and rickety. The ropes were frayed. Many of the wooden planks were missing.

"Watch out, Spider," shouted Emery as Spider scampered off. "This looks dangerous!"

Emery walked carefully onto the bridge. He tested each plank with his foot before he stepped on to it. When he reached the middle, he heard a deep laugh coming from behind him.

Dex was standing at the edge of the bridge with his sharp penknife in his hand. He started cutting the ropes of the bridge! "Ha ha, this will teach you to steal my map!" he guffawed.

Emery and Spider looked at each other in panic....

Chapter 5

Into the Water

Dex went on cutting through one of the ropes on the bridge. There was a loud twang as the rope snapped. The bridge swayed and rocked. "Give me the map and I'll let you go!" yelled Dex.

"You'll have to come and get it," Emery shouted back.

"Ooh ooh, aah aah," Spider added.

Another rope snapped.

"Quick, Spider!" shouted Emery. "We're going to have to swim for it!"

Emery closed his eyes and stepped off the edge of the bridge, pulling Spider with him. Below them, the white water rushed dangerously towards the waterfall.

"You won't get away!" yelled Dex.

Emery and Spider hit the river with a huge splash and disappeared underwater. Emery held his breath until he thought he would burst. He kicked his legs hard and fought his way back up to the surface. He was still holding his heavy rucksack.

The water crashed and smashed on the rocks.

"Spider?" he yelled. "Where are you, Spider?"

There was no reply.

"Spider?" cried Emery. "Oh, no, please…."

Suddenly there was a loud howl and Emery saw Spider at last. The little monkey paddled as fast as he could towards Emery. He climbed onto Emery's head. The two friends tried to make their way towards the bank. The waterfall was getting closer and closer.

"We're not going to make it! gasped Emery.

Chapter 6

Rescue

Suddenly, four strong arms reached down from an overhanging branch and lifted them both out of the water. They were safe.

Two men sat on the branch with them. They wore brightly coloured necklaces and skirts made of grass. Their faces were painted with stripes.

"We are Kookura people of the Amazon," said the smallest man, smiling. He bowed low. Spider scrambled up onto Emery's shoulder, chattering loudly and bowing back at them.

"Come," said the tallest man, "we can help. We will give you food and water."

Emery and Spider followed the men through the jungle back to their village.

At the village, children with painted faces ran amongst the trees. One woman in a bright headdress played music on a pipe. Another woman placed bowls of food on the table.

"Come, eat," said the small man. "We have plenty of food."

"Today is special feast day for Kookura," said the tall man. "You are our guests."

The woman laid more bowls on the table. There were tasty fish, roots and luscious fruit. A pile of bananas sat in the middle. Spider couldn't believe his luck.

By the time the feasting and dancing was over, it was very late.

Emery and Spider were tired. The tribesmen let them stay in a special little hut.

Emery and Spider went straight into a deep sleep. They didn't hear a man creeping about outside their hut in the middle of the night. They didn't hear the grass door being opened. They didn't hear someone searching through Emery's rucksack....

* * *

In the morning, they discovered that the map was gone.

"We didn't take it," said the smallest tribesman. "But look…."

There were boot prints in the mud outside the hut.

Emery looked at the tribesmen's feet. They didn't wear shoes or boots.

"Dex!" groaned Emery. "Now what do we do?"

He scratched his head. Spider scratched his head. The tribesmen scratched their heads, too.

"I know," cried Emery. "I remember. We have to head for Crocodile Canyon. We'll catch up with Dex there."

"There's only one way to get there," said the tallest tribesman. "And that's by boat," said the smallest tribesman.

"But we haven't got a boat," groaned Emery.

"You can borrow ours…." The tall tribesman pointed to a very rickety-looking raft on the river.

"Fine boat," said both tribesmen. "It hasn't sunk yet."

"OK" agreed Emery.

Chapter 7

Ferocious Fishes

The tall tribesman dragged the old wooden raft to the bank of the river. The small tribesman handed Emery a paddle.

"Good luck!" they both said.

"Let's go, Spider," said Emery to the little monkey, pushing the raft onto the river. "We must get that map back!"

Everyone waved to them as they paddled away. The green jungle slipped by on either side of the river. They heard the birds singing. They heard the monkeys in the trees. All seemed very peaceful.

Spider chattered happily to himself. He dipped his fingers into the warm water. Suddenly he let out a loud shriek. He jumped onto Emery's shoulder, trembling. The raft wobbled dangerously on the murky water. A piece of log broke off it.

"Steady, boy! What's wrong?" laughed Emery.

Spider showed Emery his finger. A large fish with big teeth was still holding onto it!

He shook his hand and the fish flew back into the river.

"Piranhas!" breathed Emery as the raft wobbled again. "Keep still, Spider. If we fall into the water, they'll eat us alive!"

Emery continued to paddle carefully. The raft moved slowly and it was hard work.

"That was close," said Emery. They entered a narrow canyon.

There were steep cliffs behind the trees on either side.

"This must be Crocodile Canyon," said Emery. "Not much further to go. Thank goodness."

Then he gasped. There was a ripple in the dark water. Two big green nostrils appeared....

Chapter 8

Crocodile Canyon

The two big green nostrils were followed by a long green nose and two beady eyes.

"Crocodile!" shouted Emery.

The raft swayed. Another bit of it broke away. But this time, it had Spider on it!

The monkey shrieked in fear. He was drifting towards the crocodile.

The huge reptile opened its jaws, its sharp white teeth sparkling….

SMACK!

Emery hit the crocodile with the paddle, right on the end of his nose.

The crocodile swam away, furious.

Emery paddled the raft to the bank of the river. Spider paddled his broken log to the bank, too. They both landed safely.

Suddenly they heard the sound of a loud voice shouting in the distance.

Dex was standing under the canopy of the trees. He was stamping his feet and shaking his fist angrily at a troop of monkeys, sitting in a tree. They were passing two pieces of paper between them.

"Give me back my map, you… you… you MONKEYS!" he shouted.

A monkey holding the map sneered down at Dex. She picked a brazil nut from the tree and dropped it onto Dex's head.

"Ouch!" yelled Dex. "That does it!"

He started to climb the tree. The monkeys leapt to the next tree. Dex tried to climb that one. The monkeys moved deeper and deeper into the forest. Dex chased after them. He didn't see one monkey slipping away from the group.

The monkey carried two pieces of paper. She swung from tree to tree until she reached Emery and Spider. Gently, she handed the map to Spider and gibbered at him.

"Ooooh, ooh, ahh," replied Spider, thanking his monkey friend for her help.

Emery and Spider put the pieces of the map together.

"Look, Spider!" said Emery, pointing in excitement. "It's just over there. X marks the spot.

That's where the Yellow Diamond of the Amazon is!"

Emery and Spider made their way through the trees. They soon reached the sheer cliff edge of Crocodile Canyon.

Ahead of them was a dark tunnel carved into the rock. Emery peered at the writing over it. He turned to Spider. "It says 'The Cave of Dreams'" he told his little friend. "I wonder what that means?"

Chapter 9

The Cave of Dreams

Emery peered into the dark cave

"Come on, my friend, let's go!"
called Emery. "We're not afraid of
a few dreams, are we?"

He pulled a torch from his
rucksack. He shone the beam of
light into the dark and eerie tunnel.

The cave at the end of the tunnel
was cold and damp. Spider shrieked

as a large droplet of water dripped from the roof onto his head. The noise echoed into the silence. They made their way carefully through the darkness. Spider held onto Emery's hand.

The light from Emery's torch suddenly fell on a huge jewel. It was perched high on a shelf in the side of the rock. It dazzled and sparkled.

"The diamond!" breathed Emery. "There it is!"

"No so fast!" called a voice in the darkness. "That diamond is mine.

All mine!" It was Dex! He stepped out of the shadows and let out a deep, bellowing laugh.

He reached forward to touch the beautiful yellow gem. Suddenly, his eyes glazed over and he stumbled.

"Ahhh," he yawned. "I feel very sleepy. I could do with a nap."

With that, he fell to the ground in a deep, deep sleep. He snored loudly.

Dex dreamed wonderful dreams. He dreamed of riches and treasures. He dreamed of being the best explorer in the world. But most of all, he dreamed of holding the

long-lost yellow diamond in his
hand at last.

"Mine, all mine…" he mumbled,
smiling in his sleep.

Chapter 10

Monkey Business

"The Cave of Dreams is working its magic, on Dex," grinned Emery. He reached out to grab the diamond. As soon as it was in his hand, though, he started to feel sleepy too.

"I think I'll just have a little lie down," he yawned.

Oh no, thought Spider. *They're both falling asleep. I'd better take over.*

Emery began to stagger and sway. He staggered forwards. Then he staggered backwards. He swayed to the left. Then he swayed to the right.

Spider leapt up and snatched the diamond – just in time. Emery stopped swaying. He stopped staggering. He woke up. "Well done, Spider," he cried. "The magic doesn't seem to work on monkeys!"

As they left the Cave of Dreams, Emery looked over his shoulder. "So long, Dex!" he chuckled to himself. "Sleep tight!"

* * *

Two days later, Emery and Spider were at the museum. They showed the precious stone to the professor. He was delighted.

Cameras flashed as reporters took pictures of them holding the sparkling yellow jewel. Emery placed the gem carefully in a display case for all the visitors to see.

Crowds cheered. Dex was there, watching. He wasn't cheering. He was green with envy.

"You won't get the better of me next time, you and that silly monkey!" he muttered under his

49

breath. "Next time, I'll find the treasure first. You just wait and see!"

THE END

FICTI🗩N
EXPRESS

THE READERS TAKE CONTROL!

Have you ever wanted to change the course of a plot, change a character's destiny, tell an author what to write next?

Well, now you can!

'Emery the Explorer: A Jungle Adventure' was originally written for the award-winning interactive e-book website Fiction Express.

Fiction Express e-books are published in gripping weekly episodes. At the end of each episode, readers are given voting options to decide where the plot goes next. They vote online and the winning vote is then conveyed to the author who writes the next episode, in real time, according to the readers' most popular choice.

www.fictionexpress.co.uk

WINNER
Education Resources
Award for Innovation

TALK TO THE AUTHORS

The Fiction Express website features a blog where readers can interact with the authors while they are writing. An exciting and unique opportunity!

FANTASTIC TEACHER RESOURCES

Each weekly Fiction Express episode comes with a PDF of teacher resources packed with ideas to extend the text.

"The teaching resources are fab and easily fill a whole week of literacy lessons!"
Rachel Humphries, teacher at Westacre Middle School

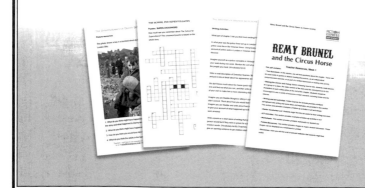

FICTI🗨N EXPRESS

Deena's Dreadful Day
by Simon Cheshire

Deena is preparing for her big moment – a part in the local talent contest – but everything is going wrong. Her mum and dad are no help, and only her dog, Bert, seems to understand.

Will Deena and Bert make it to the theatre in time? Will her magic tricks work or will her dreadful day end in disaster?

ISBN 978-1-78322-569-9

FICTI🗨N EXPRESS

The Sand Witch
by Tommy Donbavand

When twins Chris and Ella are left to look after their younger brother on a deserted beach, they expect everything to be normal, boring in fact. But then something extraordinary happens! Will the Sand Witch succeed in passing on her sandy curse in this exciting adventure?

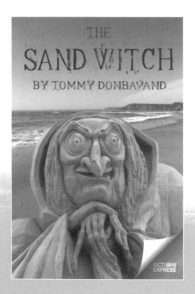

ISBN 978-1-78322-544-6

FICTI🗩N EXPRESS

Rise of the Rabbits
by Barry Hutchison

When twins Harvey and Lola are given the school rabbit, Mr Lugs, to look after for the weekend, they're both very excited. That is until the rabbit begins to mutate and decides the time has come for bunnies to rise up and seize control.

It's up to Harvey and Lola to find a way to return Mr Lugs and his friends to normal, before the menaces sweep across the country – and then the world!

ISBN 978-1-78322-540-8

About the Author

Louise John has written lots of books for children,
some to help them learn to read and some just to read
for pleasure. Usually, though, she works as an editor,
which means that she gets to help other authors to fix
and improve their stories – which is a lot of fun!
After working in publishing for many years, Louise also
taught university students all she knows about writing
and editing stories for children.

Louise lives in an old hayloft in Oxfordshire, minus the
hay, but with lots of spiders and a daughter who gives
her lots of great ideas for stories. She finds that
munching chocolate biscuits is also a helpful way to get
ideas for stories.